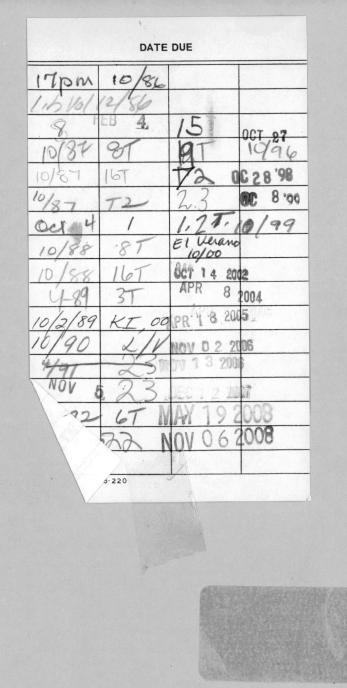

**DATE DUE**

| | | | |
|---|---|---|---|
| 17pm | 10/86 | | |
| 1.15 Vol | 12/86 | | |
| 8 | FEB 4 | 15 | OCT 27 |
| 10/87 | 8T | 19T | 10/96 |
| 10/87 | 16T | 72 | OC 28 '98 |
| 10/87 | T2 | 2.3 | OC 8 '99 |
| Oct 4 | 1 | 1.2T. | 10/99 |
| 10/88 | 8T | El Verano 10/00 | |
| 10/88 | 16T | OCT 14 2002 | |
| 4-89 | 3T | APR 8 2004 | |
| 10/2/89 | KI, 00 | APR 18 2005 | |
| 10/90 | L/V | NOV 02 2006 | |
| 4-91 | 23 | NOV 13 2006 | |
| NOV 5 | 23 | DEC 12 2007 | |
| 92 | 6T | MAY 19 2008 | |
| 72 | | NOV 06 2008 | |

6-220

# Pumpkin Pumpkin

## by Jeanne Titherington

Greenwillow Books
New York

WITH SPECIAL THANKS TO SAM

COLORED PENCILS WERE USED FOR THE FULL-
COLOR ART. THE TEXT TYPE IS ITC CASLON NO. 224
AND THE DISPLAY TYPE IS CASLON OPEN FACE.

PRINTED IN HONG KONG
BY SOUTH CHINA PRINTING CO.
FIRST EDITION
10 9 8 7 6 5 4 3 2 1

LIBRARY OF CONGRESS CATALOGING IN PUBLICATION DATA

TITHERINGTON, JEANNE.
PUMPKIN PUMPKIN.
SUMMARY: JAMIE PLANTS A PUMPKIN SEED AND,
AFTER WATCHING IT GROW, CARVES IT, AND SAVES
SOME SEEDS TO PLANT IN THE SPRING.
1. CHILDREN'S STORIES, AMERICAN.
[1. PUMPKIN—FICTION.
2. GARDENING—FICTION] I. TITLE.
PZ7.T53PU 1985      [E]      84-25334
ISBN 0-688-05695-4
ISBN 0-688-05696-2 (LIB. BDG.)

FOR
JAMES AND THE FISH

amie planted
a pumpkin seed,

and the pumpkin seed
grew a pumpkin sprout,

and the pumpkin sprout
grew a pumpkin plant,

and the pumpkin plant
grew a pumpkin flower,

and the pumpkin flower
grew a pumpkin.

And the pumpkin grew…

and grew…

and grew,

until Jamie picked it.

Then Jamie scooped out
the pumpkin pulp,
carved a pumpkin face,
and put it in the window.
But…

he saved
six pumpkin seeds
for planting in the spring.